THE SHAAR PRESS

YOUTH SERIES®

THE SEARCH FOR THE STONES

BY SHMUEL BLITZ AND MIRIAM ZAKON

ILLUSTRATED BY MARC LUMER

A SHAAR PRESS PUBLICATION

Shmuel Blitz dedicates this book
to his newest grandchild,

Eden Blitz

Marc Lumer dedicates this book
to his dear parents,

Gunter and Linda Lumer ע"ה.

And he thanks his collaborators,

K. Hartman and C. Richards

Published by **SHAAR PRESS**
Distributed by MESORAH PUBLICATIONS, LTD.
4401 Second Avenue / Brooklyn, N.Y 11232 / (718) 921-9000 / www.artscroll.com / comments@artscroll.com

Printed in Canada
Custom bound by Sefercraft, Inc. / 4401 Second Avenue / Brooklyn, NY 11232

ISBN 10: 1-4226-0934-0 / ISBN 13: 978-1-4226-0934-7

Table of Contents

A Note from the Authors

For hundreds of years rabbis, maggidim, and teachers have been using stories to teach lessons and middos.

The Search for the Stones *is such a story. Though it is not a true story, it is a story with a purpose — to teach us, through the wonders of imagination, how to act properly. We hope we have succeeded in our goal.*

Chapter 1
The Beginning

Ari and his father, Mr. Goldreich, walked back to the large square behind the Kosel to meet Ari's mom and his sister Ilana. It had been so exciting to finally see the Kosel, the Western Wall, the holiest place in the world for all Jews.

Ari and Ilana had just stuck their handwritten notes between the stones of the Wall. Their mother had told them to write down what they hoped Hashem would give them during this vacation in Israel.

"Please, Hashem, I really want to have a terrific adventure," wrote Ari.

"Please, Hashem, I'd like to meet new people and help them," wrote Ilana.

Suddenly Mr. Goldreich's cell phone rang. "I've been waiting for this call all day," he said. "Everybody stay here. I'll be right back."

At that very same moment, Mrs. Goldreich spotted an old friend she hadn't seen in years. "Don't move, kids. I'll also be right back," she said as she hurried off.

And so Ari and Ilana, for just one minute, were left on their own.

Which may not have been such a good idea — because the prayers that they had written down on their small pieces of paper were about to be answered.

The adventure of a lifetime was about to begin.

Chapter 2
The Keystone

Ari was the first to see it. It was lying there, hidden on the ground in a shady corner. "Look at this strange-looking stone," he said to Ilana, crouching down to pick it up. "It's shaped just like a key. Did you ever see anything like it?"

"Let me see," Ilana said, admiring the stone. It was shiny and glowing white. But, strangely, it sometimes changed colors, turning either red, orange, blue, or green, all in the blink of an eye.

"I wonder how it got here," Ilana said. "Do you think someone could have dropped it by mistake?"

This was Ari and Ilana's first trip to Israel. While everything they saw seemed amazing, nothing was as unusual as this key-shaped stone that kept changing colors right in front of their eyes.

Together, Ari and Ilana held the rock, marveling at its beauty. They felt a strange tingling feeling as they held it.

"I see that you have found it. That is very good," Ari and Ilana heard someone whisper behind them. Startled, they turned around, and saw an old man with a long beard standing next to them. He was dressed in a flowing white robe and a turban. He looked both kind and wise.

The two children gazed at him. "What do you mean? What did we find?" they asked.

"You have found the keystone," he explained. "It is the beginning of your search. It is the key to finding that which has been stolen — that which must be found and returned to its rightful place."

"A key? What do you mean? This is a rock!" Ari exclaimed.

"Have you lost something?" Ilana asked. "Maybe we can help you find it."

The old man smiled gently. "So many questions. So little time for answers. You will understand when you find the stones."

"Stones? What stones?" Ari and Ilana asked.

"That is your task. That is your quest. To find the missing stones. This keystone will unlock the secrets of time and space. Find the proper hole that fits this keystone, and your quest for the missing stones will begin."

"But what are we supposed to do?" Ari asked. "I don't understand."

"Four stones have been stolen, and four stones must be found," the old man explained. "They have been hidden in four different places, in four different times. You must travel through time to each of these places, find the stones, and bring them back here to me."

"How will we know where to go?" Ilana asked. "And how will we travel through time?"

"Do not worry," the old man said. "Let your faith and your pure hearts show you the way. First find the keyhole and your quest will begin. Place this keystone into the keyhole and you will be transported to the city where the first stone is hidden. It might be today, or it might be two thousand years ago. You will not know until you are there."

"Should we try the key now?" they asked.

The old man paused for a moment. "Before you begin your search, I must warn you. Since these stones were stolen, terrible things have already begun to happen. It grows worse every day. There is much danger. An evil man will be following you, trying to stop you. Even now, he is nearby and watching. But remain pure of heart, and no harm will come to you."

Ari stood tall, taking a deep breath. "We must start now. There is no time to waste."

"Yes, you must," the old man whispered. "May Hashem help you. The quest is yours. You must succeed!"

The golden-white sun shining on the stones of the plaza at the Kosel suddenly darkened. There was a warm gust of wind — and the old man was gone.

Close by, high up on a wall, a man wearing a shiny purple cape lurked in the shadows. He glared at the two children, his eyes narrowed in anger. "I must stop them before they ruin all my plans! I must!"

Chapter 3
The First Quest

Ari and Ilana stared at each other. Where had the old man gone? What had he meant by those mysterious words?

"I don't know who he was," Ari said, "but I do know that we have a job to do."

"A quest, he called it," Ilana whispered. "Ari, this is making me scared."

"Don't worry," Ari assured her. "I am here. I will take care of you."

Ilana and Ari gazed at the ancient stones of the Kosel. They had looked forward to being here. But they never, ever thought they would find such an adventure.

"Let's see now," Ari said, holding the keystone. "The old man said this will fit into a keyhole. I wonder where it is."

"Well, since we are here," Ilana mused out loud, "then right here is probably the best place to start looking."

Ilana glanced down at the floor. She noticed a small, funny-shaped crack. "Here it is!" she called out to Ari. "Right here on the ground. This must be it."

"That crack does look like a keyhole," Ari said.

"Try sticking the keystone in," Ilana said excitedly. "Let's see if anything happens."

"Okay, here goes," he replied, not knowing what to expect.

Ari stuck the keystone into the crack in the floor and slowly turned it to the right. Suddenly, they heard a howling wind so strong it lifted them off the ground. They shut their eyes in terror. Moments later, the wind grew calmer, and they cautiously opened their eyes.

Ari and Ilana gasped. They could not believe what they were seeing!

"Where are we?" Ilana asked. Her voice trembled.

"I am not sure," Ari answered, "but I do know one thing. We are not at the Kosel anymore." He looked around again. "I don't know where we are. And I'm not even sure *when* we are. This doesn't look like anything I have ever seen."

The Kosel had vanished. Ilana and Ari were standing in a field high on a hill. There were rocks and dried-up plants on the ground. Here and there a small tree provided a bit of shade. Not far away, they saw a city surrounded by a high stone wall.

"Do you think it's possible?" Ilana asked, her eyes open wide.

"I'm just not sure," Ari replied, "but I *am* sure of one thing — that city over there is Jerusalem. And I'm also sure that we have traveled far back in time, just like the man in white said. That looks like a painting of ancient Jerusalem from one of my history textbooks."

All of a sudden the children heard leaves rustling behind them. Someone was approaching. Ilana shuddered. Could it be the evil man they had been warned about?

A boy walked slowly toward them, breathing heavily. He was dressed in a colorful robe and was carrying a wooden stick.

The boy looked at them, wide-eyed. "Who are you?" he asked.

Ilana felt relieved. This boy was clearly not the evil man. "I am Ilana," she said, "and this is my brother Ari." The boy was so out of breath. "Are you okay?" she asked with concern.

Ari was not interested in how the boy was feeling. He wanted to know who he was, and where they were. "What is your name?" Ari demanded. "And what are you doing here?"

"I am Shimon the son of Yoav," the boy said, "and I feel fine, just a little worn out. It's because I've been trying to move this." He pointed to a large boulder on the ground nearby. "It's too heavy and I can't do it on my own."

"Why do you want to move that rock?" Ilana asked. It seemed both silly and impossible to do.

"Didn't you hear the story that everyone is talking about?" Shimon began to explain. "Last month a man named Rabbi Chaninah carved a beautiful giant stone to be used in the Beis HaMikdash."

"The Beis HaMikdash?" Ari shouted in amazement. "Oh, my!"

"Yes, of course, the Beis HaMikdash. That is where we go to daven and where the Kohanim bring up the offerings," Shimon said in a matter-of-fact tone. "People are always giving things to the Beis HaMikdash. Rabbi Chaninah was very poor and couldn't afford to bring something fancy, so he found a large rock and carved it. That would be his gift. But it was so big, he could not move it. He did not have enough money to pay workers to carry it to Jerusalem. This made him sad. He had worked so hard, and now he had no way to bring it to the Beis HaMikdash. Suddenly, five men appeared out of nowhere and agreed to do the job for very little money, as long as he helped them. He was delighted. As soon as he put his hand on the stone, he found himself next to the Beis HaMikdash. The men had disappeared. The Kohanim told him that the people who helped him were really angels."

"That is an incredible story," said Ilana. "Does this kind of thing happen all the time?"

"Not all the time," said Shimon, "but it sure happened last month. I know it is true because I know Rabbi Chaninah. After I heard the story, I decided that I, too, wanted to bring a large stone to Jerusalem. I have been trying all day, but it is too heavy. I can't move it. I was hoping an angel would come and help me, also."

Ilana gave Ari a look that he immediately recognized. "Yes, of course we will help him," he whispered.

"We are not angels," Ilana said, "but we will try our best to help you."

Ari was already deep in thought. "Ilana, I learned in class that when the Jews built the Beis HaMikdash they rolled the large stones that they needed from the surrounding mountains on logs, which acted like wheels. We're on top of a mountain, so we should be able to roll the stone down to the city on a few thick branches."

"You're right," she said. "Look over there. Jerusalem is not that far away. This boulder is not nearly as big as the stones they used to build the walls. I'm sure we can do it if the three of us work together."

Under the burning hot sun the three children searched the field for branches that could be used as rollers. They were so busy that they never noticed a man dressed in a purple robe, hiding in the nearby bushes, watching them.

"There," Ari said with satisfaction, wiping the sweat from his brow. "The rollers are ready. All we have to do now is shove the boulder onto them and it will go flying down the mountain. Let's just make sure there is no one in the way."

The man in the purple robe closed his eyes tightly. There was an evil grin on his face. The sky grew darker and darker.

"This weather is so strange," Shimon said, looking up at the sky. "We never have so many clouds this time of year."

"Forget about the weather," Ari said impatiently. "Let's start pushing the rock!"

As the three children leaned on the boulder, a sudden crack of thunder shattered the silence. It sounded like an explosion. Then a lightning bolt seemed to split the sky. Large white rocks rained down on them.

"Hailstones!" Ilana shrieked. "And they hurt when they hit me!"

"We have to find shelter!" Shimon cried. He had to shout to be heard over the terrifying sound of the thunder. "We'd better forget about this boulder. This plan will never work anyway!"

Ari looked at the rails that they had just finished building. It had been such hard work. If they left now, everything would be washed away by this weird storm.

"I'm not leaving," he said stubbornly. "This boulder was promised for the Beis HaMikdash, and we are going to see that it gets there."

Another blast of hail hit the ground next to them. "Have faith in Hashem," Ari cried. "He will help us succeed."

The hailstones came down harder and faster. It was like a white curtain falling from the sky. In all the commotion, no one noticed an old man with a white beard and a white robe behind a tree. The man looked at the rails the children had built and smiled.

"This cannot be allowed to happen," he thought. "Not after they have come this far, and worked so hard." He covered his eyes with his hands and lifted his face to Heaven. As quickly as it had begun, the hailstorm ended. One or two remaining hailstones fell from a perfectly blue sky, making little popping noises as they landed on the ground. Then it grew quiet and peaceful once again.

"What happened?" Shimon asked. "What happened to the storm?"

"It's just like the man in white told us," Ari exclaimed. "He said that if we have faith, we will complete our quest. Now let's get back to work!"

Shimon, Ari, and Ilana pushed and pulled the rock onto the rails. Then, with one final shove, they sent it flying down the mountain and they sped alongside. In no time it landed at the bottom, right near the city's gates.

"We did it!" Shimon shouted. "From here, I can find plenty of people to help me bring it to the Beis HaMikdash."

Ari was happy that they had helped Shimon, but he wasn't sure what to do next. "What about our quest?" he asked Ilana. "We are here for an important reason. We *must* find those stones. The man in white is depending on us."

Ilana thought back to their meeting with the old man. "He said our hearts will show us the way, and we will find the stones," she said. "I'm sure they are close by."

"What stones are you talking about?" Shimon asked. "What quest?"

Ari explained who they were and how they had gotten here, and the quest they were on.

"Funny you should talk about stones," Shimon said. "When we pushed the rock onto the rails, I saw a very unusual stone hidden underneath. Come with me and I will show you."

The three children raced back to the place where they had met. "Here it is," said Shimon. "Isn't it an interesting-looking stone?"

The stone was a deep, deep blue. It seemed to glitter and sparkle as they carefully picked it up. To Ilana, it almost seemed that it was smiling at them. *But that was silly*, she thought. *Stones can't smile. And yet ....*

"It's the first stone!" Ari shouted gleefully. "We found it."

"You know," Ilana said thoughtfully. "If we hadn't helped Shimon, the stone would have stayed under the boulder that he couldn't budge. We would never have found it. Maybe that's what the old man meant when he said we should be pure of heart and have faith, and we would succeed. We were able to find the first missing stone because we helped Shimon."

"Yes. Of course. That must be what he meant," Ari agreed.

Shimon looked puzzled. "I still don't understand too well what it is you're looking for. But I know that *I* was looking for angels, and found the two of you instead. You don't look like angels, but you sure helped."

Ari looked more serious than usual. "Help doesn't have to come from angels. Hashem can send help in many different ways. Sometimes it can even come from your friends. I guess we are now your friends."

"Ari, look there," Ilana exclaimed. "Do you see that funny-looking hole next to the stone?"

Ari smiled. "I wonder, if I stick the keystone into it ...?"

Before he did, they said goodbye to Shimon. "I hope you succeed in your quest," he said, as he walked toward the city to deliver his boulder.

Ari and Ilana waved until he was down the mountain. Then, Ari took the keystone from his pocket. He stuck it into the hole and turned it to the right.

Again they heard the howl of the powerful wind as their feet rose off the ground.

And their quest continued.

Chapter 4
The Second Quest

This time, the key did not take them to a mountaintop. This time, the two children found themselves in a place that was completely, absolutely…

"Dark! It is so cold and dark in here," Ilana said. Ari could sense the fear in her voice.

"Yes, it is. But don't be afraid." Ari was a little frightened himself, but he tried to sound confident. "The man in white told us that if we stay pure of heart and have faith, we will be safe."

"I can't see anything," Ilana whispered. "And do you hear all that shouting and screaming above us?"

"I do, and it is making me a little nervous also," Ari said.

Slowly their eyes adjusted to the darkness.

"Look over there. It's a tiny window," Ari said.

"It has bars on it!" Ilana exclaimed. "Are we are in some kind of prison?"

"That is exactly where you are. You are in a dungeon," a voice said. A young boy emerged from the shadows and approached the two children. "Who are you? When did they bring you in here?"

"It's a long story," Ari replied. He was not yet ready to tell a stranger where they were really from. "Who are you?"

"My name is Fernando," the boy replied, "and sitting on the floor in the corner is my sister, Angelina."

"My name is Ilana, and you just met my brother, Ari. Where are we?"

"Don't you know? We are in the dungeon of the King and Queen of Spain," Fernando explained. "We were brought here a few days ago. You two must have been thrown in some time during the night, while we were asleep."

"Why are you here?" Ilana asked.

"Probably for the same reason you are. Because we are Jews. Do you realize that in a few moments we will all be brought before Torquemada?"

"Torquemada?" Ari asked in astonishment. "But he was the head of the Spanish Inquisition. He was the Grand Inquisitor who had so many thousands of Jews killed."

"He *was* the Grand Inquisitor?" Fernando's voice sounded bitter and rough. "Why do you say 'was'? He *is* the Grand Inquisitor. He was the Grand Inquisitor yesterday, he is today, and unless Hashem helps, he will still be tomorrow."

Angelina rose from the dirty and dusty corner. "They are new here and they have no idea what they will be facing," she said to her brother. "Please explain this to them in a kind way. What we say to others and how we say it is very important."

"You are right, my sister. Listen to me, Ari and Ilana. Both of you must be very careful when you speak. Torquemada will twist your words and turn everything that you say against you."

Ari grew pale. He knew that this was a very bad time in Spain for the Jewish people. The King and Queen had decreed that Jews must become Christians or else flee the country. Some Jews pretended to become Christians, but kept the Torah in secret. When the Inquisition discovered them, the evil Torquemada had them severely punished. Many were even put to death!

If it was Torquemada that they would be facing, they were in very serious danger!

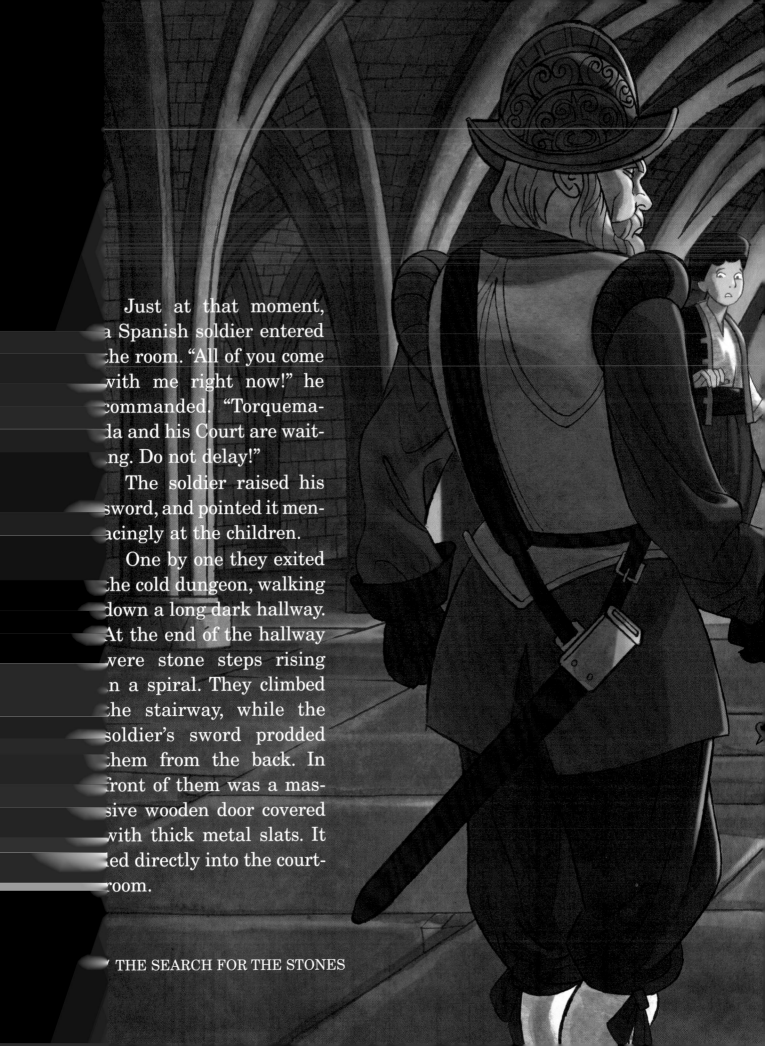

Just at that moment, a Spanish soldier entered the room. "All of you come with me right now!" he commanded. "Torquemada and his Court are waiting. Do not delay!"

The soldier raised his sword, and pointed it menacingly at the children.

One by one they exited the cold dungeon, walking down a long dark hallway. At the end of the hallway were stone steps rising in a spiral. They climbed the stairway, while the soldier's sword prodded them from the back. In front of them was a massive wooden door covered with thick metal slats. It led directly into the courtroom.

The soldier opened the door. They entered and heard a loud voice call out, "All members of the court, be seated!"

The children saw a man in a black robe seated behind a wooden table. It was Torquemada himself. Surrounding him were many soldiers holding spears. Ari and Ilana were so terrified by the sight that they hardly noticed the man sitting next to Torquemada. He had bushy black eyebrows and wore a purple robe.

"Ah, I see we have young children with us today," Torquemada remarked, an evil smile visible on his face. "The church always takes pity on children. Let us see what the charges are against them. Ah, yes. A very serious charge, indeed. It seems that you children have been keeping the Jewish Sabbath!"

Fernando and Angelina looked at each other. They were shocked. They had always been so careful to keep Shabbos in secret. How could the Inquisition have found out?

Torquemada stared at them. He seemed to know just what they were thinking.

"You wonder who told us, do you not?" he shouted. "I will tell you. It was your good friend, Doña Gracia! And by chance she is here today in court."

A soldier nudged an old woman forward with his sword. She looked frightened and forlorn.

Angelina stared. "Doña Gracia? Our neighbor? Our friend?"

Torquemada laughed wickedly. "Your friend? Yes. She is a friend with a big heart, and even a bigger mouth." He looked at the papers in front of him. "She saw people coming to your house, one by one, on the Jewish Sabbath. She told her neighbor, Doña Sofia, how nice it was that you children entertain guests in your house. Doña Sofia mentioned it to her mother-in-law, Doña Maria, who spoke to her husband, Don Henrique, who told his son, the soldier and good Christian, Juan Hernandez — who told the Inquisition. And now here you are. So much talk, just to snare a few Jewish souls."

Torquemada was no longer laughing. He appeared to be growing angrier and angrier by the moment.

"Last week Juan Fernandez entered your house and found these items hidden under the sofa." He held up a pair of *tefillin*. "Do you have anything to say about all this?"

Fernando looked at Angelina. Then they both stared at Doña Gracia, who was now in tears. She had caused so much trouble by speaking without watching her words. Fernando knew nothing would be gained by responding, so he kept quiet, hoping his sister would do the same.

"I want to save you," Torquemada now said in a low and gentle voice, "but I cannot do it without your help. I will send you to the monastery. The priests will be nice to you. They will educate all of you to be good Christian children."

For the first time, the man in the purple robe sitting next to Torquemada began to speak. He shot up from his chair and shouted cruelly, "No. This cannot be. The four of them must be killed immediately. These Jews cannot be allowed to live even for one more day."

"Do not worry, my good friend," Torquemada replied. "I have no doubt these children will meet their fate shortly. But for now, let the priests have them. Now, away, all of you. I have important business to attend to!" He clapped his hands, and a group of soldiers surrounded the children and led them from the courtroom.

The walk to the monastery was very short. Six priests met them at the front gate and brought them inside.

"I am so afraid," Ilana whispered to Ari. "Back at the dungeon I feared for my life, but here I fear for my soul."

"Don't worry," Ari answered gently. "We will escape from here, and with our help Fernando and Angelina will also go free."

The priests led the children into a room containing many scrolls and manuscripts. "Children, we are here to help you," one priest began. "We are here to save you. We will teach you to become good Christians and then you will have a good life in the care of the Church."

"We are Jews. We are not Christians and we will not become Christians," Fernando shouted. "Do not try to make us convert. You cannot!"

"We only wish to talk to you," the priest said. "But most important, you must give us the names of other Jewish children whom we can also help."

"We will not tell you anything," Angelina said firmly. "We have nothing to say. We will never give you the names of other children, and we will not listen to what you have to say to us!"

"Then your stay here will be brief and bitter," the priest sneered. "Take them upstairs," he commanded another priest. "Perhaps if we starve them for a while they will be more cooperative."

The other priest led them up a flight of stairs to the second floor, where they were placed in a small, dark room. There wasn't much in it, just a bed and a few rickety chairs. He left and carefully bolted the heavy wooden door behind him.

Then, Ari gathered everyone together. "I have an idea how we can escape. Tonight, when the priests are all asleep, we will tie these bedsheets together and use them as a rope to climb down from this window."

"Excellent," Fernando responded. "Let us rest now, so we will be awake to escape tonight."

That night there was a full moon in the sky. Jackals howled in the distance. The children worked feverishly to tie the sheets together. Finally, Ari bound the end of the last sheet tightly to the bedframe that he had already moved to the window.

"I will go first and make sure it is safe," Ari offered. "Then Ilana and Angelina will climb down and Fernando will go last."

One by one the children grasped the bedsheet rope and slowly made their way down the wall. Ari, Ilana, and Angelina were already on the ground when suddenly they heard a ripping sound.

"The sheet is tearing from the weight," Fernando whispered, his voice filled with panic.

The next moment, he landed on the ground with a loud thud. "Let's get out of here quickly," Ari commanded. "That noise probably woke some of the priests."

The four children sped to the entrance gate. Ari pushed open the heavy metal door. They heard shouts from behind, so they broke into a run.

"The children are escaping!" one priest yelled. "Everyone, after them. We cannot let them get away!"

"Angelina and Fernando," Ari called. "Run into the forest. Ilana and I will distract them. They will chase after us and the two of you will escape."

"We cannot leave you," Angelina and Fernando both said. "We will all stay, and meet our fate together."

"No!" Ari ordered, trying to take charge. "Don't argue with me. I have a plan. Run now and run quickly! Don't worry. We will be safe."

Angelina and Fernando fled into the woods. Ilana and Ari ran in the other direction, making sure the priests saw them. The priests chased after them, enabling the other two children to get away. Spotting a cave, Ari said, "Ilana, let's hide in here. That way, it will take them longer to find us."

The priests continued searching and eventually found them in the cave. Two priests grabbed them by their arms. "Where are the other two?" one priest bellowed. "Tell me now!"

"We will not tell you," Ilana answered softly. "We will never tell you."

"Then the two of you can go back to the dungeon to die. Let Torquemada deal with you as he wishes. I wash my hands of you Jews," the priest said in disgust.

The children were led back to the same cold dark dungeon where they had met Fernando and Angelina. "I hope Fernando and Angelina got away," Ilana said.

"I am sure they did," Ari said quietly. "Fernando told me of a boat leaving this week, that is traveling far away over the ocean. Their family knows the captain, and they were planning to join him on that boat. The name of the captain is Christoforo Columbo. That's Christopher Columbus!"

"Oh my," Ilana said. "In that case, I have no doubt they will get away safely. But what about us? Are we going to be stuck in this dungeon forever?" She began to cry.

"Don't be scared," Ari assured her. "I let the priests capture us so that Fernando and Angelina could get away. Remember, if we have faith, we will be saved. I have faith. I trust in Hashem."

An old man with a white beard stood outside the dungeon. He gazed in through the small window. "This just will not do," he said quietly. He covered his eyes with his hand.

All at once, a thin gleam of light danced through the tiny window. In its beam the two children saw the dirty floor and the dank, damp stones of the walls. They could see a filthy pile of hay that was provided to prisoners for use as a bed. And they saw one more thing.

"Look!" Ilana shrieked. "Look at that beautiful green stone!"

The deep green of the stone looked even more splendid against the dirty dungeon floor.

Ari snatched the green stone and placed it into his pocket, alongside the blue one. Then he carefully withdrew the keystone. He crouched down and pushed away the dust that had surrounded the stone. And there it was — a crack in the rock that looked just like a keyhole.

"Where do you think we will end up next?" Ilana asked. She sounded worried.

"I don't know," Ari answered, as he gently eased the keystone into the crack. "But one thing is for sure. It's got to be better than this place. Ready? Here we go!"

He shut his eyes and turned the key to the right. In a twinkling the dungeon was empty. Ari and Ilana were gone.

Chapter 5
The Third Quest

ri and Ilana were free. The cold dark dungeon was gone. They found themselves standing next to a placid blue river under a shining yellow sun.

"This is a lot nicer than where we just were," Ilana said with a smile. "I could get used to being here."

"Let's not get too comfortable," Ari said. "We are here for a purpose. We have a quest to finish."

Ilana nodded. Turning around, she noticed two boys who seemed to be Ari's age. They were acting strangely. Both were standing in the water almost up to their waists, each holding a pan. They would dip the pan into the stream, shake it, look at the pan, and then dip it again.

"Ari, what do you think they are doing?" she asked. "Let's go over and ask them."

"I guess that will be the best way to figure out where and when we are," Ari replied. "They seem safe enough."

They walked over to the boys. "Good afternoon," Ari said with a smile. "Can I ask what you are doing?"

"The same thing everyone else here is doing," one of the boys answered. "Looking for gold. Don't you know where you are?"

Ari was not yet ready to tell them too many details. He just said, "Actually we are a little lost and not exactly sure where we are."

"Then welcome to Sutter's Mill," the boy laughed. He waded out of the river and Ilana noticed that his pants were torn and dirty. "Now that you know where you are, you'd better start looking for gold just like everyone else."

Sutter's Mill? Ari thought. *I learned about Sutter's Mill in school. We must be in California during the Gold Rush. Thousands of people went there in the 1800s, looking for gold.* He turned back to the boys. "Can you tell me what year it is?" he asked.

"That's a strange question," the boy replied. "It's Monday, June 4th, 1849. My name is Sol and this is my younger brother, David. What are your names?"

"Sol and David?" Ilana asked. "Are you Jewish?"

Sol grinned. "Yes, we are."

Ari was surprised. "There are Jews here?"

"Our family left Russia five years ago," David said. He looked sad as he spoke. "Our ship docked in New York, but life was very hard for us. So six months ago our parents decided to pack up everything we owned and go west looking for gold. But they both died on the way."

A tear rolled down David's cheek. "So now it's just the two of us, me and my brother, Sol."

"All by yourselves?" Ilana was shocked. "Then who takes care of you?"

"We take care of ourselves. Out here, no one takes care of anyone else," Sol explained. "They only care about gold, gold, and more gold. Nothing else interests them. But we manage just fine."

Ilana looked at the two boys. They didn't look like they were managing fine at all. Their faces were pale and they were very thin.

"You know, we are Jewish also. My name is Ilana and this is my brother, Ari."

"Really? We don't meet too many Jews here."

"How do you look for gold?" Ari asked, changing the topic.

"The two of you must really be new to these parts," Sol laughed. "What we do is called 'panning.' You see this pan? We dip the pan in the water and fill it with gravel and mud from the river. We hope that there will be tiny pieces of gold hidden in the mud. Gold is heavier than the mud, and will sink to the bottom of the pan, so we tilt the pan on its side, and let the water and mud run out of it. Then, we look and see if there are any stones left in the pan. If we are lucky, we find gold."

"We can lend you a couple of pans if you'd like," David added. "We have extras there by the side of the stream. Then you can also pan for gold."

"Have you found any gold?" Ari asked.

Sol gave a short laugh. "Not much. Lots of stones, but not much gold."

Ilana took a deep breath. "They're finding stones!" she whispered to her brother. "Ari, maybe we'll find the next missing stone in this river. Maybe that's why we are here!"

A few minutes later, Ilana and Ari were standing in the cold water next to their new friends. Only they were not looking for gold, they were searching for the third stolen stone.

It was hard work, and Ilana soon became tired. She took a break to rest her arms, and asked Ari if he wanted to join her.

"No," he said, not even looking up. A short while later, he turned to her and said, "I've got a great idea. Let's separate, and look in two different parts of the river."

Ilana noticed a funny glint in Ari's eyes. He seemed to be very far away. "I don't want to separate," she replied. "We always stay together."

"If we separate," he answered, "we will have a better chance of finding gold."

"Gold?" Ilana exclaimed in shock. "We are not looking for gold! We are looking for the stolen stones. What do you mean by gold?"

"Did I say gold?" Ari laughed sheepishly. "I meant the stone. Yes, of course. We are looking for the stone. You stay here, and I will go looking farther up the stream, where there is more room."

Ilana was not happy. Ari had never behaved like this before. He hardly heard what she said.

The river was crowded. Thousands of people had come to the area when they heard that gold had been found there. Ari had to walk upstream quite a way until he found a place where he was alone.

He dipped his pan into the river, tipped the pan to let the water run out, and looked to see what remained.

"Hello, sonny," Ari heard someone say. He did not even turn around to see who it was. He was checking on the stones in his pan.

Ari felt a finger tap him on his back. Its touch was cold. He turned and saw an old prospector. The man had bushy eyebrows and wore a purple vest and a purple hat.

"Having any luck today?" the man smiled. But the smile was as cold as the man's icy finger.

He looked familiar, but Ari had no idea where he had seen him before.

"Gold is an amazing thing," the man in purple said. "If you've got enough gold you can buy anything. You can do anything."

"What do you mean?" Ari asked.

"Well, I figure everyone has a different use for money. Some people just want to go out and have a good time. Others want to buy lots of things. And people like you want to do good deeds with their money. I figure that you probably want to help people — like those two boys you just met."

For a moment Ari wondered how this man knew about Sol and David. Before he could ask him, though, the man spoke again.

"The only way to get more gold is to keep looking for gold," the man advised. "If you really want to succeed, you have to stop everything else you are doing, and just keep working hard to get more gold."

Ari thought of all the gold he could find. He thought of how much good he could do with it. *Yes, that's it. If I pan enough gold, I could help people, like those two boys.* He imagined a mountain of gold nuggets piled high in front of him. *I will keep working hard to get more gold. That's the most important thing.*

He turned back to the river, and didn't notice the old prospector walk away. The man had a big smile on his face. A cold and chilling smile.

Darkness was falling. Ilana wondered where Ari was. She began walking upstream along the bank of the river. "Ari, where are you?" she called over and over. A few minutes later, she found him standing knee-deep in the water.

"Ari, why didn't you answer when I called? And what are you doing here so late? It's getting dark," she said impatiently.

"I know, but look how much gold I found," Ari replied, proudly showing her a large pile of shining nuggets. "I need more time. I need more gold!"

"More gold?" Ilana shouted. "We are not here to find gold. We are here to find the missing stone! What's gotten into you?"

"I need to find more gold, so I can help David and Sol," Ari replied. "And the only way to get more gold is to keep looking for gold." His voice sounded strange.

"You are fooling yourself," Ilana told him sternly. "You are not looking for gold to help them. We can find adults to help those two boys. You are gathering all this gold because you have become greedy like so many of the others here. I even see the change in your eyes."

Ari ignored her, and once again began panning for gold. Ilana slowly walked away. *I don't understand what's happened to him,* she thought. *What could have caused him to act like this?*

"What's the matter?" Sol asked, when Ilana had returned. "And where is your brother?"

"I don't understand." She burst into tears. "Ari is not acting like himself at all." Ilana then told the two boys who they were, where they were from, and their quest to find the missing stones.

"That is amazing," Sol said, not fully believing her story.

"Here. Take this. It is for the two of you," she told the brothers as she handed David a rock. "While panning for the missing stone, I found this nugget of gold instead. I have no use for it, and I want you to have it."

The two brothers' eyes opened wide. The gold nugget was huge. It would buy enough food and clothing to last a long time. "Thank you so much. In all the time we have been here, no one has tried to help us. Not even once," Sol said. "You are such a kind person."

"Where I come from, we call this *tzedakah* — charity. It's the right thing to do," she explained.

"You can't imagine how much your gift means to us," David said. "Today, Sol and I spent the entire day panning for gold, and all we have to show for it is this pile of worthless rocks."

"This nugget is going to buy us many dinners," Sol said. He tossed it happily into the air.

It was already dark. The nugget gleamed in the moonlight. It cast a beam onto the mound of stones lying on the riverbank. In its light, Ilana saw that one of those stones was a deep, dark ruby red.

"Look at that one in the corner," she shouted. "That is the next missing stone. You found it! Do you think I could have it?"

"Of course. Why not?" David said. "It's not gold. We don't need it."

Ilana gently picked up the ruby-red stone and ran to where Ari was still panning for gold in the dark. "Look Ari. I found it," Ilana panted. "We have the next missing stone. Now we can leave here and continue on our quest."

Ari turned and grimaced at Ilana. "I can't leave now," he said, showing her the gold he already had. "If I stay here another few days I can find even more gold."

"But Ari, we are here for a purpose. We are here on a quest, not to get rich. We are here to find the stolen stones," she said in frustration.

"I want more gold! I don't care about the missing stones," Ari shouted.

As soon as those words left his mouth a cold wind began to blow. All the camp-fires along the river-bank grew dark. The only light came from the shining full moon.

First there was silence. The wind stopped as suddenly as it had started. Then Ari and Ilana heard the sound of giant wings flapping. A terrifying screech split the

night, as a flock of ravens and vultures circled overhead.

"What's that noise?" Ilana shouted in terror.

Ari looked confused and frightened. "What have I done?" he whispered.

Suddenly, from high above in the sky, Ilana saw a giant purple cloak fly down. It looked like it was being carried by the ravens themselves.

Ari disappeared into the folds of the cloak.

And then he was gone.

Chapter 6
Captured in the Cave

Where am I?" Ari whispered. "It's so cold. Is there anybody here?"

"You are in a cave deep under the ground," an icy, sinister voice replied. "Now you are in *my* power. Now, you are under *my* control."

In the dim light, Ari could barely make out the figure of a man wearing a dark purple robe. "Who are you?" Ari asked. "You look so familiar. How did I get here?"

"None of that is important right now," the man answered. "The only thing that is important is the stones."

"I don't understand," Ari said. "I am on a quest and I have one more stone to find. I must get back to my sister right away."

"Your quest is over," the man said. "You cannot leave. There is no escape. There is no entrance and there is no exit." An evil smile appeared on his face. "But we can be friends," he continued. "I am willing to make a deal with you. If you give me the stones that you have already found, I will allow you to return to your precious sister."

"I cannot do that," Ari said. "I told the man in white I would find the stones and give them to him."

"Then you will remain buried in this cave forever," the man in the purple robe hissed. "You have just one hour to decide. I am placing this box in the corner. If you want to be reunited with your sister, you will put the stones in that box. If not, you will never leave this cave alive."

There was a burst of cold wind, a strange purple mist filled the room, and the man in the purple robe was gone.

Ari sat down on the ground and stared at the small iron box in the corner.

What will I do? he thought. *If I don't give that evil man the stones, I will be stuck here forever, all alone.*

Then he heard a quiet voice in the darkness. "Ari, you are never alone. No one is ever all alone."

"Who is that?" Ari asked with a start.

Then he saw a ghostly white figure in the darkness. It was the old man who had sent them on their quest! He came closer and sat down next to Ari. "You are never alone if you have faith in Hashem," he said.

"What does that mean?" Ari asked.

"Do you remember when you and Ilana began your quest?" the man in white asked. "I told you that you must be pure of heart to complete it and to remain safe. And I also told you that you must have faith."

"Yes, of course I remember," Ari replied.

"Then think about how you acted today," the old man explained. "You gave up on your quest for the stolen stones. Instead you went searching for gold. You were no longer pure of heart."

"You are right," Ari admitted. "But what can I do now? I am trapped here forever."

"As long as you are alive, you are never trapped anywhere," the old man continued. "There is no problem that cannot be solved. There is no place that a person cannot escape. You only need to find the proper key to leave."

"I have the keystone," Ari said. "Can I use it to escape?"

"No, I am sorry, but you cannot," the old man said sadly. "Your keystone will only work if you are pure of heart."

"But I want to be pure again," Ari cried. "How can I do that?"

"You will know the answer by yourself," the old man said. "The knowledge is within you." And with that he was gone.

Now Ari felt truly alone in the dark cave. Tears rolled down his cheeks. "Why did I act so badly today? Why did I let the gold take control over me? Why was I so mean to my sister? I want to be pure again," Ari called out, though he knew no person was there to hear him. "I will not make that same mistake again. And I will not help that evil man in the purple robe."

Ari stood up and yanked all the gold nuggets out of his pocket. "Why did I even take these? They are all worthless!" he screamed.

He walked to the corner of the cave, opened the iron box, and threw the gold nuggets in. "Here, you can keep this gold. But you will never get the stones!" he shouted as he kicked the box.

The iron box moved a few inches. Underneath it, Ari saw a hole in the ground. The hole was shaped like a key.

"The keyhole!" he gasped.

Ari felt a burst of happiness that seemed to light up the dark cave. Now he could escape from the horrible man in the purple robe. But even more, he knew that, once again, he was pure of heart.

And most of all he was happy because he knew that the old man was right. He was never alone, not as long as he had his faith.

Ari pulled the keystone from his pocket and placed it into the hole. He turned it slightly to the right, felt a gust of wind lift him off the damp ground, and he was gone.

Chapter 7
The Fourth Quest

Ilana sat by the riverbank, her eyes filled with tears. Her brother was gone. He had disappeared into a giant scary-looking purple cloth. The keystone was gone with him, and she had no idea if she would ever see him again, or how she would get home.

A gentle breeze made ripples on the river. And then, just as suddenly as he had vanished, there was Ari, standing in front of her. "Ari, what happened to you?" Ilana shouted. "I was so worried! Are you okay?"

Ari looked around nervously. "We have to get out of here as quickly as possible. Do you have the stone?"

"Yes. I have it right here," Ilana answered, showing him the ruby-red rock. "Let's go back to the campsite. The keyhole must be there under the pile of rocks where I found this. We can say goodbye to Sol and David, and be on our way."

"Yes, but let's hurry," Ari said. "I want to get as far away from here and the man in the purple robe as I can."

Ari and Ilana hastened to the campsite where David and Sol were preparing dinner. "Ari, we were so worried about you," Sol said. "Are you okay?"

"I'm fine, I think," Ari said. "But now, we must say goodbye to you and be on our way."

"Ari, there it is," Ilana interrupted. "The keyhole. I knew it would be by that pile of stones."

Ari quickly took the keystone from his pocket and stuck it into the hole. He turned it to the right, and then, with a giant rush of wind, the two were gone.

Ilana and Ari opened their eyes. "I bet Sol and David are still standing there with their mouths wide open," Ilana said with a chuckle. "I

don't think they believed me when I told them where we were from and the quest we were on."

"Well, I'm sure they believe you now," Ari smiled. Here, far away from Sutter's Mill and from the dark cave, he finally felt safe and calm.

"I gave them the gold nugget that I found," Ilana told him. "I hope it helps them."

"I don't ever want to hear about gold again," Ari said. He felt ashamed of himself. "I definitely learned my lesson." He told his sister the story of what had happened to him while he was trapped in the cave.

"I would have been terrified," Ilana said quietly.

"I really was. I was so scared. But I did learn a lot from the man in white," Ari added. "And now, just where, and when, are we?"

They looked around. They had arrived in a city filled with skyscrapers. Old-fashioned cars were being driven down the road.

Across the street, they saw a boy their age, kicking a soccer ball against a wall. "Let's ask him," Ari said. "Maybe we will figure out where the last stone is, and how we can get it. I can't wait to get back to the Kosel and see Abba and Imma."

But before they could approach the boy, he came over and began talking to them. "Will you play soccer with me?" he asked. "I have no one else to play with."

"Actually, we are kind of busy right now," Ari replied. "But could you please tell me where we are?"

"First of all, what are your names?" the boy asked. "My name is Menachem Cohen, but my friends call me Manny."

"I am Ari, and this is my sister, Ilana."

"Hi. Welcome to Brasilia, the new capital of Brazil. I arrived here from Israel two weeks ago with my father. My mother got sick, so she had to stay behind, but she will join us soon. In the meantime, it's just me and my little sister, Esther, and I'm bored. My father is very busy. He looks for bad people all day, so he doesn't have much time for me."

Ari noticed a man selling newspapers on the corner. He saw the date on the front page. It was Tuesday, June 4th, 1963.

"What kind of bad people does your father look for?" Ilana asked curiously.

"He looks for Nazis," Manny said quietly. "They were German soldiers who killed millions of Jews during World War II. Many of their leaders were caught, but after the war some Nazis escaped from Germany and came here to Brazil. I heard my father say that there is a very bad Nazi right here in this area."

"If your father is so busy, and your mother is still in Israel, who takes care of you and your sister all day?" Ilana continued.

"My dad sends his driver, Pedro, to watch us," Manny explained. "He is very nice. Look over there. He is coming here now with Esther."

Ari and Ilana saw a man exit the front door of a tall building. A four-year-old girl was at his side. The man was dressed in a neat beige jacket, with matching beige pants that were perfectly pressed.

"Manny, would you like to come with us to the park?" Pedro asked, a big smile creasing his face.

"Yes," Manny said. "Can I bring along my new friends?"

"Of course. Why not?" Pedro replied.

Manny and Esther skipped to the park, smiling and laughing. Manny was so happy to have found new friends with whom to play. Behind them Ari and Ilana walked together. They were both deep in thought. "I don't even know where to began searching for this missing stone," Ari admitted.

"The keystone has always brought us to the right place," Ilana replied. "Maybe we are supposed to help Manny's father find the Nazi. Maybe that's why we were sent here."

"I've already seen pure evil in the cave. I saw it in the eyes of the man in purple," Ari shuddered. "I'm not sure I'm ready to start dealing with any nasty Nazis right now."

Ilana walked toward the swings in the park, while Ari stood in a corner watching the others. Esther was playing with Pedro near the fountain in the center of the park. "Look how high I can jump," Esther giggled.

She jumped higher and higher. Then, lying in the mud next to the fountain, something interesting caught her eye. She made a move to pick it up and slipped, landing on the ground with a huge splash. Mud went flying in every direction. A large chunk splattered Pedro's pressed beige pants.

Pedro glared at Esther. His blue eyes burned with rage. "I will kill you!" he shouted. "Look what you did to my pants!"

Esther burst into tears. "What happened?" Manny called, running over to see what the commotion was all about.

"He yelled at me," Esther whimpered. "I thought he was my friend."

"I'm sure it was an accident," Manny told Pedro, while Ilana helped the crying little girl to her feet and tried to comfort her. Manny turned to Ari. "You were watching. She didn't do it on purpose, did she?" Ari didn't answer. He just stood there. His face was white.

Pedro took a deep breath. "Yes, you are right," he said. "I never should have lost my temper. I am sorry." With that, they all began walking to the apartment building.

"Ari, what's the matter with you?" Ilana asked. "You look like you've seen a ghost."

"No, not a ghost," Ari whispered. "Much worse than a ghost. I've seen pure evil again."

"What are you talking about?" Ilana asked.

"I saw Pedro's eyes when he screamed at Esther," Ari whispered. "It's one thing to lose your temper, but this was much worse than that. I saw that same look in Torquemada's eyes, and I saw it in the man in the purple robe. Pedro is evil! Evil through and through!"

Pedro entered the building, while the four children lingered outside, not sure what they should do. A few minutes later he emerged, carrying

a small suitcase. He walked quickly to a car parked on the side of the road, jumped into the driver's seat, and roared off. He didn't say a word to any of them.

"I wonder, where is he going in such a hurry?" Ari asked Manny.

"Let's go upstairs and ask my father," he replied.

The children climbed the two flights to Manny and Esther's apartment. "Abba, these are my new friends, Ari and Ilana," Manny said. "Where did Pedro rush off to?" he added.

"Nice to meet you," Mr. Cohen said to Ari and Ilana. "Pedro told me he just received a call that his aunt was very sick, and he needed to go see her. I told him it was okay."

Ari took a deep breath. "I don't want to be rude, Mr. Cohen," he said, "but I don't think he is telling the truth." He told him how Pedro had lost his temper in the park. "He didn't even have time to get a phone call from anyone. Besides …" he hesitated.

"What is it?" Mr. Cohen asked. "What is bothering you?"

"I saw the look in his eyes when he was screaming at Esther. He's a bad man, Mr. Cohen. I don't think he can be trusted."

Mr. Cohen was quiet for a minute. He looked carefully at Ari. Then he seemed to make a decision. He sprang up from the sofa and hurried to the telephone. "Now it all makes sense," he said, quickly dialing a number.

"I couldn't understand how those men always knew where I was going even before I got there," he muttered, after he had hung up. "At last I understand. Pedro was the spy." Mr. Cohen's face was grim. "I've sent my men to follow him."

They sat together in the apartment, waiting for news of Pedro. One hour passed and then the phone rang. "Yes, yes, I understand," Manny's father exclaimed into the phone. "Keep trailing him, but don't do anything until I get there."

"What happened?" Ari asked.

"One of my men just told me that Pedro is driving toward the Amazon rainforest. I have an intelligence report from my government that says there is a Nazi hideout there. I will head there now and investigate. You stay here. I will call a neighbor to watch you. She'll be here soon."

With that, Mr. Cohen sped from the apartment.

Little Esther didn't understand what was going on, but she was still upset that Pedro had screamed at her. "All I wanted was to pick up this pretty stone," she pouted.

Ilana and Ari immediately turned to the stone in Esther's chubby hand. It was bright orange and it seemed to wink at them.

Ari gave Ilana a knowing look. "It has to be the last missing stone," he murmured.

"Esther, can I look at that?" Ilana asked. "You found this by the fountain in the park? It is so beautiful. I wish I had one just like it."

Esther smiled. "You can keep it if you like. I have plenty of other toys."

Ilana took the stone, trying to hide her excitement. "Ari and I have to go now," she said, just as the neighbor walked in to watch the two children.

Ilana and Ari rushed to the fountain in the park. "This is it," he said. "The final stone. Our quest is over. Now we can go back to the Kosel!"

"And back to Abba and Imma," Ilana added with a smile.

In the mud near the fountain, the two children saw the keyhole. Ari took the keystone from his pocket and placed it into the hole. A quick turn to the right, followed by that same strong wind, and they were gone.

The next moment they opened their eyes, but they were not where they expected to be.

"Where are we?" Ilana asked. "Why aren't we back at the Kosel?"

Ari looked around at the

thick trees and high grass. He heard the sound of a strange bird screeching. The air was thick, hot, and wet. "I don't know. It looks like we are in some kind of rainforest," he said.

"I'm scared," Ilana shivered. "There may be snakes and wild animals here."

"It's not the wild animals we need to worry about," Ari said quietly. "It's them." He pointed to a group of four or five men talking nearby.

"It's Pedro!" Ilana exclaimed.

"It's worse than that," Ari said somberly. "It's Pedro and the Nazis."

Chapter 8

In the Rainforest

Pedro and the Nazis! They were standing a few yards away, in front of a small wooden hut in the middle of the forest.

"We can't let them see us," Ari whispered, "but we must get closer so we can hear what they are saying." Silently, the two children crawled along the ground, hiding under the giant leaves and trees. They were now just a few feet from the men.

"Our Leader will be arriving soon," Pedro began. "Let's go into the hut and wait for him." Pedro looked nervous. He kept glancing over his shoulder. Sweat dripped down his face.

After all the men entered the hut, Ilana and Ari crept to an open window to hear what they were saying. It was quiet inside. Then after a few minutes, two jeeps arrived. A man who was obviously the Leader stepped out of the first jeep, along with three others. Four more emerged from the second jeep. Still hidden by the underbrush, Ari and Ilana watched as the eight men rushed into the hut.

The Leader began to speak. "Today will be remembered forever! It is a historic day." he declared. "It is true that World War II is over, and we Nazis were not victorious. But we lost only the first battle. We did not lose the war. The real war is only now beginning! Right here, from the Amazon Rainforest. Revenge on the world will be ours!"

Ilana and Ari stared into the window. A horrified look appeared on Ari's face. "That's him!" he whispered.

"Who?" Ilana whispered back.

"Do you see that man in the purple uniform standing next to the Leader? He's the man who took me prisoner in the cave."

The Leader finished his speech. Everyone in the room cheered. Pedro slowly raised his hand, looking even more nervous than earlier. "I am sorry to report, sir, that I think I've been discovered. It was those children …." His eyes blazed with fury. Ilana wondered how they had ever thought he was a nice man. "I think I was followed here," Pedro continued. "I suspect the Israelis will arrive within the hour."

The Leader scowled at Pedro. His face twisted with rage. Then the man in the purple uniform whispered a few words into his ear. A cold smile returned to the Leader's face. "Do not worry, my dear friend Pedro. This is a good thing. The bridge is just a few minutes down the road. We will go there now, and place bombs under it. When the Israelis drive onto the bridge, it will explode and blow them up. I have grown tired of their interfering with my plans."

Pedro looked relieved. That is, until the Leader spoke again.

"Of course, these bombs are a bit tricky. You never know if they will detonate while they are being set in place. You, Pedro, will have the honor of handling them. Now, everyone follow me!"

The Leader walked to his jeep and lifted out two dark square blocks of metal nestled on the back seat. "These, my friends, will take care of the Israelis. They are weight-sensitive bombs. They do not explode until at least 500 pounds are on top of them. Unless, of course, someone makes a mistake while attaching them. That will be Pedro's job. When the Israelis drive over the bridge, these two bombs will explode, killing them all."

Everyone smiled as they walked in single file toward the bridge. Ari and Ilana followed at a safe distance. "Pedro, come and put them in place," the Leader commanded. "The rest of you, stand back. Do your job well, Pedro, and you will be forgiven for allowing the Israelis to follow you here. That is, if you survive," he smirked.

Slowly, carefully, Pedro attached the bombs to the underside of the bridge. When he was finished, he stood up. He was covered with sweat. His hands were shaking. But he was alive!

"Our work here is done," the Leader announced. "Let us now return to our headquarters and make our plans. The Nazis will rise again!"

Ari and Ilana waited quietly while the men returned to the hut. "We must get in touch with Mr. Cohen and his agents before they get to the bridge," Ari stated. "We must warn them about the bombs." He began walking quickly down the jungle path toward the bridge.

"But Ari," Ilana protested. "For us to meet Mr. Cohen, we have to walk over the bombs ourselves!"

Ari closed his eyes for a moment. Then he stood up straight. "You heard him. The bombs will only explode when something heavy sets them off." He tried to smile. "Neither of us weighs 500 pounds. I'll go first," he said, as they reached the rickety wooden bridge.

Ilana held her breath as she watched Ari carefully cross the bridge. Then, with a prayer in her heart, she stepped on the wooden slats. One step, two, three, four …. There! She was safely past the bombs!

As soon as they had crossed the bridge they heard the sound of car engines. Three jeeps were speeding down the road, coming right toward them.

"Come, Ilana. Quickly!" Ari shouted. "It must be Mr. Cohen and his men. We've got to stop them from reaching the bridge!"

Closer and closer, the jeeps approached. Ari and Ilana jumped into the middle of the road, right next to the bridge, waving their arms and shouting. The children knew it was dangerous, but they had no choice. If the jeeps didn't stop right away, they would be blown up!

The driver of the first jeep blinked. He wondered if he was seeing a mirage. There, in the middle of the rainforest, right in front of him, two children were jumping up and down, wildly waving and shouting!

He slammed on the brakes. There was a terrible screeching sound, as the jeep skidded to a halt, just inches from the children.

"Stop!" the two children shouted. "There are bombs under the bridge."

Mr. Cohen was the first to jump out of the jeep. "What in the world are you two doing here?" he demanded. He was shocked to see his son's friends in the rainforest. "How did you get here before us?"

"There is no time to explain," Ari said. "We must act quickly. You cannot drive your cars onto this bridge, because the Nazis put bombs under it. It will explode when something heavy, like a jeep, passes over it."

Mr. Cohen looked shocked. "The Nazis are already here?" he asked.

"Yes," Ilana answered quietly. "There are about 10 or 12 of them. Pedro is here too. He warned them that you were coming. That is why they put the bombs under the bridge."

Mr. Cohen smiled grimly. "Okay, so they wanted to ambush us? We'll ambush them instead!" He turned to his men. "We can still cross the bridge one at a time. You, Rafi," he said, pointing to one of the men, "will remain back here."

"But I don't want to miss the action," Rafi protested.

"Believe me, you'll be making more noise than any of us," Mr. Cohen laughed. "Here is my plan …"

Keeping absolutely quiet, Mr. Cohen and his band of Israeli agents crossed the bridge, one at a time. Ari and Ilana followed. After arriving on the other side, they looked around, staring at the giant trees of the rainforest.

"Okay, up we go," Mr. Cohen announced. The men climbed up and hid in the thick green leaves of the trees. Ari climbed also, and pulled Ilana after him.

Mr. Cohen then leaned out of his tree and waved a handkerchief so that Rafi, the Israeli who had remained on the other side, could see it. Rafi leaned into the jeep that was closest to the bridge. Carefully, he started the engine and gave the jeep a shove. Then he ran and hid behind a massive boulder, while the jeep rolled onto the bridge.

Ari and Ilana stared out from the greenery. Suddenly there was a giant explosion! The empty jeep had set off the bombs! Ilana put her hands over her ears, while Ari watched the bridge go up in flames.

As Mr. Cohen had expected, all the Nazis raced out of their wooden hut. They were eager to see how they had destroyed the Israelis.

"We got them!" the Leader shouted.

"Not quite!" said Mr. Cohen, as he leaped from the tree, right on top of the Leader himself. The other Israelis also jumped and wrestled the remaining Nazis to the ground.

Within minutes, the Nazis were tied up, prisoners of the Israeli forces. Only one had escaped. No one knew how, but the man in the purple uniform had vanished without a trace.

Mr. Cohen went over to Ari and Ilana. "The two of you are the heroes of the day," he said. "If not for you, we would have all been killed, and they would have succeeded in forming their new Nazi group."

"We were happy to help," Ilana smiled.

"I have just one question," Mr. Cohen added. "When I left my apartment, the two of you were there with my children, Manny and Esther. And when I arrived here, you were waiting for me, helping to save our lives. How did you get here so fast?"

Ari and Ilana both grinned. "If we told you, you wouldn't believe us. We will go back to Brasilia with you, and then be on our way."

The group took the Nazis' jeeps and drove several miles down the road to another bridge, where they crossed the river. Ari and Ilana returned with them, while the prisoners sat sullenly in the back of the jeeps, their wrists in handcuffs.

When they were finally back in Brasilia, Ari and Ilana said their goodbyes to Mr. Cohen and his children and walked to the park.

"I just figured out why we didn't arrive back at the Kosel when I put the key into the keyhole before," Ari explained. "Our quest was not just to find the stolen stones. We were given a mission — to help people. We could not leave Shimon in Jerusalem until we helped him move his stone to the Beis HaMikdash. We could not leave Spain until we helped Fernando and Angelina escape from Torquemada and the Inquisition."

"I see," said Ilana, her eyes opening wide. "And we could not leave California until we helped Sol and David by giving them the gold nugget I had found."

"And we could not leave here until we helped Mr. Cohen destroy the Nazis," Ari continued. "Now, I guess, we are finally ready to go back to the Kosel."

"I sure hope so," Ilana agreed. "I really miss Abba and Imma."

Brother and sister walked toward the fountain and Ari took the keystone out of his pocket. He placed it in the keyhole, turned it to the right, and ... the two children were gone.

Chapter 9
Return of the Stones

A moment later, Ari and Ilana opened their eyes. In front of them was the holy Kosel.

They were back at the plaza near the Wall, right where they had started.

"Yay! We did it!" Ilana gushed. "We made it back!"

"And we finished our quest," Ari added. "We have the four stones for the man in the white robe. I wonder how we will find him."

There was a light gust of wind. Ari felt a warm, friendly hand touch his shoulder. "I am right here with both of you, as I have always been," the man in white said. "You two have done a magnificent job. I am very proud of you."

"Here are the stones," Ari said, a wide smile across his face.

"It is hard for me to explain how important it was to find these stones," the old man told them as he gently placed them into a small brown sack. "So much bad could have happened. Now I can return them to where they belong."

"But there is so much I don't understand," Ari said. "I have so many questions for you."

"Questions, answers, questions, answers. So many questions, so many answers," the old man replied mysteriously.

"When I was in the cave," Ari asked, "the man in the purple robe could easily have taken the stones from me. Yet he told me to leave them for him in the iron box. Why didn't he just grab them from me?"

"That is an easy question," the old man answered. "That man is very evil. Evil such as his cannot touch these stones. They would destroy him. He needed you to put them in the iron box, so that he could take them away without touching them."

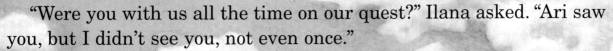

"Were you with us all the time on our quest?" Ilana asked. "Ari saw you, but I didn't see you, not even once."

"Yes, of course I was with you. Remember, I told you that if your hearts remained pure and you had faith, you would succeed. Ari, you had so much faith when you helped Shimon during the hailstorm. And you both kept your hearts pure when you helped Fernando and Angelina escape from Torquemada."

"But after that, I acted badly at Sutter's Mill," Ari said. A tear rolled down his cheek.

"That is true," the old man agreed. "But you learned from your mistake and felt very sad about what you had done. That can often make a bad deed totally disappear. Ilana was so pure of heart when she helped Sol and David. And you both showed great courage when you helped Mr. Cohen capture the Nazis." The man in white gave the children a proud, happy smile.

"You fulfilled your quest," he continued, "and you rescued these stones. And you both learned some very important lessons."

"Here is the keystone," Ari said as he took it from his pocket. He gave a little sigh. "I am sure going to miss it."

"I suspect that one day you will be using it again," the old man said with a twinkle in his eyes. "And remember: The quest was yours. And you have succeeded!"

A warm gust of wind blew past them, and the old man was gone.

And far overhead, a dark purple raven watched and waited.

Mr. Goldreich finished his phone conversation. He turned around and saw his children standing at the other end of the Kosel plaza. *I hope they weren't too bored waiting for me,* he thought.

Mrs. Goldreich said goodbye to her friend and returned to Ari and Ilana. "It's time to go home, kids," she said. "I think we've done enough for one day."

"We sure did," Ari answered. He smiled at his sister.

Ilana smiled back and said, "Yes, we did!"

Glossary

Abba — Father.

Beis HaMikdash — The Holy Temple, which was located in Jerusalem.

daven(ing) — pray(ing).

Don — (Spanish) Mister.

Doña — (Spanish) Mrs.

Hashem — G-d.

Imma — Mother.

Kohanim — the descendents of Aharon, the brother of Moshe Rabbeinu. They performed the service (special duties) in the Beis HaMikdash.

Kosel — (also **Kotel**) the Western Wall, the holiest place in the world for all Jews because it is the last remaining part of the wall that surrounded the Beis HaMikdash.

maggidim — speakers or lecturers who use stories to teach their lessons.

middos — here, positive character traits

Shabbos — (also **Shabbat**) the seventh day of the week, which G-d commanded us to keep holy.

tefillin — the two square leather boxes containing Torah passages written on parchment and worn by Jewish men during Shacharis, the morning prayers.

Torah — a parchment scroll containing the Five Books of the Bible (Chumash).

tzedakah — charity.